"Go home," said the fish. "Now she is back in the hut." And there they are still living to this day.

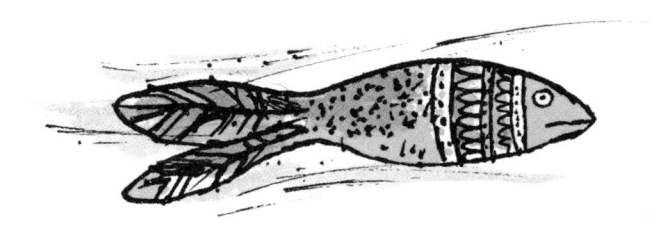

away. Outside a storm was howling, and the wind blew so hard that he could scarcely keep on his feet. Thunder shook the mountains and rocks rolled into the sea. Great black waves, all crested with white foam, surged and crashed. The fisherman shouted at the top of his voice, but could not hear his own words:

> *Oh magical fish,*
> *Oh fish in the sea,*
> *Pray, grant the wish*
> *That my wife begs of thee!*

"Well, what does she want now?" said the fish. "Alas," said he, "she wants to be like God."

"Husband," she said, kicking him with her foot, "wake up! Go to the fish, for I wish to be like God."

The fisherman was still half asleep, but he was so horrified at what he heard that he fell out of bed. He rubbed his eyes and said, "Wife, what are you saying?"

"Husband," said she, "if I cannot command the sun and moon to rise, I can't bear it. I shall not know another happy hour. Go at once!"

Then she fell into such a rage that without a word the fisherman pulled on his trousers and ran

Thereupon they both went to bed, but she could not sleep, for she was constantly thinking what there was left for her to be. At length the sun began to rise, and when the woman saw the light of dawn, she sat up in bed. She said, "Why can't I, too, command the sun and the moon to rise."

"Wife," said the man, looking closely at her. "Are you now pope?"

"Yes," she said, "I am pope."

"Good," said he, "now that you are pope, you will be satisfied. You cannot become anything greater now."

"I will think about that," said the woman.

So back he went, and when he got there he found a large cathedral surrounded by palaces. He pushed his way through the crowd and saw his wife clad in gold, sitting on a much higher throne. And she had on a crown encrusted with jewels. Emperors and kings were on their knees before her.

"Well, what does she want now?" said the fish.

"Alas," said the man, "she wants to be pope."

"Go to her, then," said the fish. "Now she is pope."

The fisherman was so afraid that he shivered and shook and his knees trembled. But he went to the fish. A high wind blew clouds across the sky, and the water churned and roared, and waves pitched and tossed his frail craft. Full of fear and despair, he cried:

> *Oh magical fish,*
> *Oh fish in the sea,*
> *Pray, grant the wish*
> *That my wife begs of thee!*

"Husband," said she, "why are you standing there? I am not content to be emperor; I will be pope. Go back to the fish."

"Oh, wife," said the man, "is there no end to your wishing? You cannot be pope; there is but one pope in all Christendom."

"Husband," said she, "go at once. I must be pope this very day."

"No, wife," said the man, "it is impossible. I dare not say that to the fish. He can't make you pope."

"Nonsense!" said she, "if he can make an emperor he can make a pope. Go to him. I am the emperor; obey me!"

Barons and counts and dukes went about the halls, while his wife sat on a high throne of gold with a great golden crown on her head. She held the sceptre in one hand and the imperial orb in the other; and on both sides of her stood soldiers of the imperial guard with gleaming swords.

The fisherman approached the throne and said, "Wife, are you emperor now?"

"Yes," said she, "now I am emperor."

Then he stood and looked at her for some time, and said, "Dear wife, be content, now that you are emperor."

Oh magical fish,
Oh fish in the sea,
Pray, grant the wish
That my wife begs of thee!

"Well, what does she want now?" said the fish.

"Ah, fish," said he, "my wife wants to be emperor."

"Go to her," said the fish. "Now she is emperor."

So the fisherman went, and when he got there found a palace made of polished marble with alabaster figures and doors of solid gold.

So he was forced to go. But he was very uneasy, and thought to himself, "It will end badly; it will end badly! Emperor is too shameless! The fish will be angry this time."

He found the sea black and murky, boiling and bubbling up from below, and dark clouds were filling the sky. He was frightened, but still he said:

Inside everything was of marble and gold, with velvet covers and great golden tassels. His wife was sitting on a throne with a golden crown on her head and a jeweled sceptre in her hand, and she was attended by maids-in-waiting.

The fisherman stood before her and looked at her for some time. Then he said, "Ah, wife, now you are king."

"Yes," said the woman. "Now I am king."

"And now that you are king," he said, "let things be. Don't ask for anything more."

"No, husband," said the woman, "I find that time passes very slowly when one is only a king. Go to the fish and tell him I must be emperor."

"Oh, wife, why must you be emperor?" said the man. "There can be only one emperor in the land. The fish cannot make you emperor. Surely he cannot."

"What!" said the woman, "I am the king, and you are nothing but my husband; go at once! If he can make a king he can also make an emperor. I will be emperor. Go!"

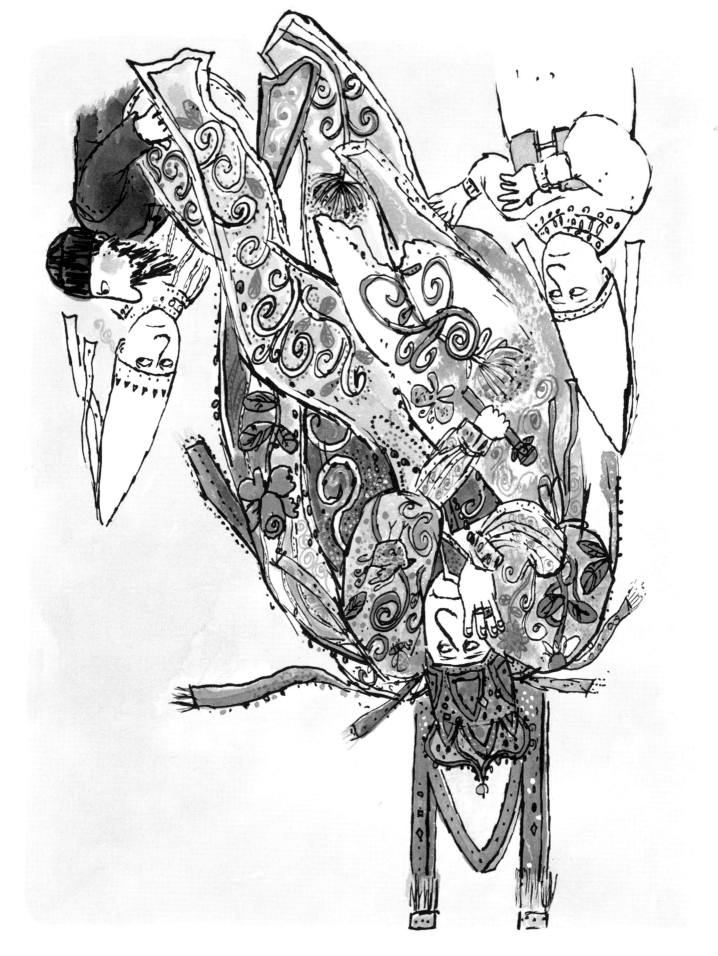

So the fisherman went, and what he found was no longer a mansion but a great castle with a high tower and soldiers standing guard before the door.

When he came to the place in the sea, it was dark gray and the water heaved and swirled, and a wind was blowing. The fisherman raised his voice and said:

Oh magical fish,
Oh fish in the sea,
Pray, grant the wish
That my wife begs of thee!

"Well, what does she want now?" asked the fish.
"Alas," said the man, "she wants to be king."
"Go to her; now she is king," said the fish.

Next morning at daybreak the wife awoke, and from her bed she saw the beautiful country that lay beyond the gardens and orchards which surrounded the mansion. She poked her husband in the ribs with her elbow, and said, "Get up, husband, and look out of the window. Why can't we be the king over all that land? Go tell the fish to make us king."

"Alas, wife," said the man, "why should we be king? I do not want to be king."

"Well," said the wife, "if you won't be king, I will. Go ask the fish; go this instant!" So the man went, but he was quite unhappy that his wife wished to be king. "It is not right," he thought. "It is not right."

and said, "Come in." So he went in with her, and found a great hall paved with marble. Servants flung wide the doors and they went through rooms filled with richly carved furniture; and carpets covered the floors, and crystal chandeliers hung from the ceilings.

"Now," said the woman, "isn't that grand?"

"Yes, indeed," said the man, "now let it be. Let us live in this beautiful mansion and be content."

"We'll see," she said. Then they went to bed.

The fisherman went home, and when he got there
he found a great stone mansion. His wife was standing on the steps, and she took him by the hand

"Well, what does she want now?" said the fish.
"Alas," said the fisherman, half scared, "she wants
to live in a great stone mansion."

"Go, then," said the fish. "Now she has it."

The man's heart was heavy. He said to himself, "It's not right." But finally he went. When he came to the place in the sea, he found the water still quiet, but grown quite thick and gray. He looked at it and said:

Oh magical fish,
Oh fish in the sea,
Pray, grant the wish
That my wife begs of thee!

Everything went well for a week or so, and then the wife said, "Listen, husband, this cottage is far too small for us. The fish might just as well have given us a larger house. I should like to live in a great stone mansion. Go to the fish and tell him to give us a mansion."

"Wife," said the man, "this cottage is good enough. Why should we live in a mansion?"

"Never mind!" said the woman. "Just go to the fish and tell him."

"No, wife," said the man, "I don't like to go back to the fish so soon. It might make him angry."

"Go along," said the woman, "he will be glad to do it."

When the man went home, his wife was no longer in the hut. In its place stood a pretty cottage, and she was sitting on a bench before the door. She took him by the hand and said to him, "Just come and look inside. Isn't this better?" So they went in and there was a parlor and a bedroom with brightly painted furniture, and a kitchen and pantry fitted up with beautiful things made of tin and brass. And behind the cottage was a yard with hens and ducks, and a garden with flowers and vegetables.

"Look," said the wife, "isn't that nice!"

"Yes," said the husband, "now we will live quite contented."

"Perhaps," said the wife. With that they ate supper and went to bed.

"Go, then," said the fish. "Now she has it."

When he got to the place where he had caught the fish, the water was no longer clear and smooth. He looked down into the green and yellow depths and said:

Oh magical fish,
Oh fish in the sea,
Pray, grant the wish
That my wife begs of thee!

Then the fish came swimming up and said, "Well, what does she want?"

"Ah," said the man, "my wife says that since I caught you, I ought to have wished for something. She does not want to live in a hut any longer; she wants a little cottage."

"Husband," said the woman, "have you caught anything today?"

"No," said the man, "I did catch one fish, but he said he was an enchanted prince, so I let him go again."

"Didn't you wish for anything first?" said the wife.

"No," said the fisherman. "What should I have wished for?"

"Ah," said the woman, "isn't it disgusting to have to live in this miserable hut? You might have wished for a little cottage for us to live in. Go back and call the fish. Tell him that we want a little cottage. He will certainly give us that, since you caught him and let him go again."

The man did not want to go back there, but his wife kept urging him, and he didn't like to oppose her. So pretty soon he returned to the sea.

fisherman," it said, "let me live. I am not really a fish, but an enchanted prince. I would not be good to eat. Put me back in the water and let me go!"

"Yes," said the fisherman, "you don't have to plead with me. I will certainly let go." And with that he put the fish back into the water and watched it swim to the bottom. Then the fisherman went back home to his wife.

and he fished, and he fished. One day he was sitting with his rod, staring into the clear water, when his line suddenly went down, far down below. When he pulled it up again there was a large fish hooked on the end. At once the fish spoke, "Hark, you

NCE UPON A TIME there was a fisherman who lived with his wife in a miserable hut near the sea. Every day he went out fishing;

AND HIS WIFE

From the story The Fisherman and His Wife by Jacob and Wilhelm Grimm

THE FISHERMAN

BY MARGOT ZEMACH

W · W · NORTON & COMPANY · INC · New York

For
Julia and Hans